# BÊTE NOIRE

## FEAR IS JUST A POINT OF VIEW

Editors:

A. W. Gifford

Jennifer L. Gifford

www.betenoiremagazine.com

Bête Noire is published by Dark Opus Press a division of Charm Noir
Omnimedia

ISBN-13: 978-0-9985931-0-4

ISBN-10: 0-9985931-0-9

Film Studies by J.J. Steinfeld first Published in Grain Magazine
Roses and Ivy by Diane Arrelle first published in Dark Valentine, 2011

# In This Issue

# Film Studies

## J. J. Steinfeld

There are two uniformed police officers in the brightly lit room, and they are big men. The uniforms look rather old-fashioned, but appear to be freshly laundered, crisp. I'm sitting at a sturdy old wooden table, in an uncomfortable, rigid chair; the two men standing over me, looking more bored than menacing. Both of them look like bodybuilders, have huge necks, brush cuts and steely blue eyes. I think they might be brothers, and I ask them that. The police officer chewing his gum like there is no tomorrow laughs, then says they are distant cousins. The other one says they are kissing cousins, and the first one pantomimes a few punches to his partner's jaw.

The second police officer begins to scratch his head, his fingers working as fast as the other police officer's jaws. I make a remark about the gum-chewing police chief in the great 1967 film *In the Heat of the Night,* and both policemen say they have never heard of that movie. I tell them that this semester one of the courses I'm teaching is on the films of Norman Jewison, and they tell me they have never heard of a punk like me teaching in any school. They laugh at what I was saying. I'm a visiting professor of Film Studies, I explain, and I'm finishing my stay in New York. I'm going back to Toronto in two weeks. They tell me I'm not going anywhere, let alone escaping over the border.

Both policemen light up cigarettes at almost the same time. Surprised, I ask if smoking isn't banned in the building and they look at me as if I'm saying breathing is outlawed. There are three ashtrays on the table I'm sitting at. The gum-chewing, big-necked cop asks me if I want a cigarette, and I tell him I don't smoke, never have.

"A punk like you never smoked? Hell, I have a hard time believing you're a clean liver," the head-scratching, big-necked cop says.

"So, why'd you do it, kid?" the gum-chewing cop asks.

"All I did was jaywalk," I say, doing my best not to start hurling insults at the two big men. "Why'd you bring me here?" I ask with annoyance and impatience.

"Jaywalking, he calls it. What kind of joke talk is that?" the head-scratching cop says. "Let's hear a confession and we can go home. I'm sure the judge will appreciate it. Skinny, pimply-faced punk like you ain't going to have a happy time in the slammer."

"People don't go to jail for jaywalking," I protest. The cabbie, I recall, had to slam on his brakes, and I apologized, but he let go with some colourful language. I smiled in the face of his profanity-laced harangue and told him that Toronto cabbies express themselves more eloquently. But there were no police officers around when that happened this morning. And what is with the skinny and pimply-faced description? I pat my overweight belly and rub my bearded face, putting the lie to the policeman's ludicrous description. I tell myself I need to get more exercise, watch what I'm eating. When I get back to Toronto, I promise myself, I'm going to resume my morning and evening walks. Double the distances. After the first few weeks in New York, I haven't been doing much walking.

"Those are beautiful vintage uniforms," I comment, trying to get my thoughts off my health, and the two policemen look at each other's uniforms, touch each other's sleeves mockingly. "You commemorating some kind of anniversary? But why isn't there a detective questioning me?"

The gum-chewing cop holds his sleeve right under my nose, rubbing back and forth not too lightly, and says, "I don't think any detectives would want to waste their time with a punk like you. Kid, you're going to the Big House for a long time if you don't cooperate. Why'd you do it?..."

Why are they calling me a punk and referring to me as a kid? I'm over fifty years old and these policemen look like they'd be in their late twenties, maybe early thirties. And what is with this "Big House" routine? These two guys seem to be delivering their lines straight from a corny script parodying a melodrama. And where did they get the old-fashioned police uniforms?

I stand up and the gum-chewing cop sits me back down with a firm press of his hand. "No funny stuff, kid..."

"This is like an absurdly bad movie," I say, tapping at the table in an attempt to conjure up some sanity and reasonableness.

"I like the movies," the head-scratching cop says.

"Me too. Saw me a neat double feature last Saturday," his look-alike partner follows.

"You guys both remind me a little of Stallone, younger versions, of course. Rambo and Rocky Balboa."

"Who is that we remind you of, kid?" first one of the policemen says, and then the other: "Never heard of any of them, punk."

"You guys are putting me on. Sylvester Stallone played Rambo and Rocky Balboa in some of the most successful box-office films in history. Real tough guys." I feel like I'm talking to two students who have missed all the semester's lectures and now I have to explain the most rudimentary aspects of film to them.

"James Cagney and Edward G. Robinson, those are my idea of tough guys," the head-scratching cop says.

"I like old films also," I say, hoping that maybe these guys will lighten up and stop this silly charade. I've discussed several of Cagney's and Robinson's films in one of my courses. Is there a better scene than Cagney heading for the electric chair in *Angels with Dirty Faces*? During a lecture last month I compared the execution scene in that Cagney film with the one in *Dead Man Walking*, and the acting styles of Cagney and Sean Penn. I wince at the memory of myself imitating Cagney for my students.

"You should have gone to the picture show yesterday, punk, then you would have saved yourself all this trouble." First one policeman and then the other finishes his cigarette and puts it in the ashtray closest to me.

"I was just going to a ball game. I was in a hurry. I'd already missed the first inning."

"What ball game might that be, punk? Dodgers, Giants, or Yankees? You look like a Bums' fan. Am I right?"

"Naw, he's a Giants' fan. I'd put money on that."

"So, punk, what's the team?"

"I was going to see the Mets play the Diamondbacks. I'm a Blue Jays fan back home, but I've gone to quite a few Mets games while I was teaching here."

"What the hell are you talking about, kid?"

"You think we're stupid, punk? You think you can sit here and make fools of us? You're going down, punk. The Big House is gonna be your home address until your hair turns good and grey..."

My hair is already grey, for God's sake, and I rub the sides of my head as if trying to make my thick, dark hair reappear from a decade or two ago. I think of the film *The Big House* and ask the two police officers who starred in it and what year it came out, a snap quiz. They look puzzled and don't even attempt a guess. I tell them Wallace Beery, 1930, and one policeman says he was in short pants when that movie came out.

"Why'd you do it?" the other policeman asks.

"It isn't a crime being a Mets fan. My mother, believe it or not, is a Yankees fan, which is most peculiar. How many seventy-eight-year-old little old ladies in Toronto root for the Yankees? She never paid any attention to baseball when I was growing up. It's only since —" I stop abruptly and look around the room; I really didn't want to talk about her condition to these two strangers.

"At least your momma has taste, kid."

I watch the two police officers, look for something in their eyes or gestures that will betray them, expose the act they are putting on, but the way they speak and behave doesn't seem like acting, only strange, enormously strange. They are treating me as though I'm a rambunctious teenager. I want to be in the classroom. I have a class on film to teach. I ask to see a mirror.

"What you want to see your ugly kisser for, punk?"

I jump up and run for the door, but the gum-chewing cop blocks my way. "Trying to escape is not going to make the judge soft-hearted with you," he says, and leads me roughly back to the table.

"You've been on *Law & Order*, haven't you?" I say, as I sit back down, trying to regain my composure.

"What's that, punk? More of your crazy talk?"

"My favourite TV show."

"You start talking square with us, or else I'm gonna be even more unhappy with you."

"If you don't like *Law & Order*, I can't help it. What, you into *NYPD Blue*?"

"What the hell is TV? Some secret code of yours? You a spy for the Germans, punk?"

"Doesn't look like a Kraut lover, but you can never tell."

"I'm Jewish."

"Did you know we had us a little kike?"

I protest the derogatory term, accuse these two men of going overboard, and the head-scratching cop calls me a sensitive little Yid, while the other one pinches my shoulder and says, "I like Hank Greenberg, even if he swats all those homers for the Tigers. Good hitter, no deny-ing that."

"Greenberg is one of my all-time favourite Hall of Famers."

"You gotta be retired, kid, to get into the Hall of Fame. Any ball fan knows that. You get a jumbled head?"

"I rented the DVD last week — *The Life and Times of Hank Greenberg*. Fabulous documentary."

"What did you rent?"

"*The Life and Times of Hank Greenberg*."

"No, those initials."

"A DVD."

"I don't know what you're talking about."

"You still into video cassettes? You're really missing out."

"I don't like your code. Speak English."

They both light up another cigarette, back to their synchronized smoking team. The smoke is like out of a bad movie, but I've already thought that. Or a good *film noir*. Black and white. I tell them again that I teach Film Studies. I start rattling off my favourite *films noir*, as if they might bring these police officers back to reality, to shatter their asinine little game. They look at me completely perplexed, shaking their heads at my comments. They have been doing a lot of head-shaking at what I've been saying.

I plead with them to stop smoking. I'm getting a headache. I search my jacket pockets for my cellphone. I better call the Film Studies De-partment and let them know I'll be a little late for class. "What'd you do with my cellphone?" I ask angrily. I feel like my connection to the outside world had been severed.

"You got your own punk language, don't ya?"

"You have your own idiotic phoniness."

"Watch your lip, punk."

Still searching through my pockets, I realize my wallet is also miss-ing, and my keys. "You guys pickpockets in your spare time?"

"You'll get your possessions back later. No one's going steal your crummy things from us."

"My students are getting restless right about now. I don't want to miss my class."

"This is your last chance, punk. We're going to lock you up. That old guy had a heart attack when you broke into his house..."

I was fifteen when that happened. I hit a ball through a window. I just went to get the ball back. No one was home. The only person who knew was my brother. But that was in the late 1960s, not in the early 1940s that these two police officers are pretending to be part of.

"My brother died years ago," I state, sure that will shatter the farcical scene these men are trying to maintain. One of the last conversations I had with my brother was about baseball, the same night we'd gone to a Blue Jays game together. I can't remember who the Blue Jays had played, or who won, and the memory lapse annoys me.

"Not what we heard. But we're not talking about your brother now. We'll be talking to him soon enough. Once we catch him. Your parents aren't gonna be happy with their lawbreaking sons."

"My father was proud of both of us, believe me. We were both there when he died, holding his hands." I resist telling my persistent interrogators that my father was much more of a hockey fan than baseball, was disappointed that neither my brother or me showed much skating ability, and I get lost in the deathbed memory scene.

"Who you trying to sucker? We know where your parents live."

"My mother has Alzheimer's," I blurt out, leaving my father's dying, feeling that these two characters are going much too far.

"Only thing she has is a double-talking punk of a son sitting in front of me and a scared punk son hiding behind some garbage can somewhere."

"You guys have some very odd and erroneous information," I say, emphasizing my point and dislike of the smoking with a some theatrical coughing. Between some of my emphatic coughs, I demand, "Give me my cellphone!"

"Okay, punk, we've been nice enough with you. You can tell your cellmates all those things you been rambling at us, and see how they like it. Maybe your cellmates like cellphones."

The head-scratching cop opens the door and the gum-chewing cop lifts me up from my seat and leads me out of the room. I'm in a police station, except it looks like a set from an old movie, maybe a James Cagney or Edward G. Robinson movie. As I walk past a glassed-in office I see my face. My fifteen-year-old face. "It was an accident," I scream. "My brother pitched me a curve ball and I fouled it into a neighbour's window. There was no one home..."

"Slap the cuffs on this punk. I think he's been spending too much time hiding out at the picture show, trying to learn to be a mean, trouble-making gangster," one policeman tells the other.

"I want out of this bad movie," I shout, trying to sound as tough and confident as Edward G. Robinson, and wait for the two police officers

to tell me they are actors playing a joke, put up by some of my col-
leagues in the Film Studies Department, maybe even some of the more
diabolical students, but the police officers are acting deadly serious,
and as the gum-chewing, big-necked cop grabs me from behind and
the head-scratching, big-necked cop puts the handcuffs on my wrists,
tightening them, I yell in pain, wishing I could change this frightening
script.

*Canadian fiction writer, poet, and playwright* J. J. Steinfeld *lives on Prince
Edward Island, where he is patiently waiting for Godot's arrival and a phone
call from Kafka. While waiting, he has published seventeen books, including*
Disturbing Identities *(Stories, Ekstasis Editions),* Should the Word Hell
Be Capitalized? *(Stories, Gaspereau Press),* Would You Hide Me? *(Stories, Gaspereau Press),* Misshapenness *(Poetry, Ekstasis Editions),* Identity
Dreams and Memory Sounds *(Poetry, Ekstasis Editions),* Madhouses in
Heaven, Castles in Hell *(Stories, Ekstasis Editions), and* An Unauthor-
ized Biography of Being *(110 Short Fictions Hovering Between the Absurd
and the Existential, Ekstasis Editions). More than four hundred of his short
stories and eight-hundred poems have appeared in anthologies and periodicals
internationally, and over fifty of his one-act plays and a handful of full-length
plays have been performed in Canada and the United States.*

# WICKED CABARET

## D. B. Heath

Fresh blood pours from the tap,
Served with demon wings on a torso platter
While the bartender shakes her spear-headed tail
For undisclosed tips.

The faceless stripper struts down the stage
To tease perverted minds for the main event.
With paraphilic fantasies the vixen dances,
Tying the strings of bed puppets
That wait for a private encore
To enter her canyon of tourists and trespassers.

The rowdy crowd at the Wicked Cabaret
Is full of misfits and neurotic dreamers;
Damned souls in eternal filth,
Among Hell's festival of freaks and gore.

Burlesque goblins with devil sticks,
Phantom sword swallowers
And headless hula-hooping hermaphrodites
Parade around a boisterous audience
While the Marlboro zombie hides behind cigarette smoke;
A fearsome bouncer with intimidating hunger
Waiting for agitators to be swallowed
As eidolons scream for the next performance.

The Nightmare Nymphs take the stage
Dressed in unkempt leather,

Hypnotizing like stars of a gothic planet
As they sing their songs of dark elegance.
The crowd roars to the blasting beats
Of The March of Imps and Boomerang Bullets
With vicious excitement.

The sinister and surreal entertainment,
Heard from miles away,
Mocks the angry and sorrow dead
On the streets of the abyss.

D. B Heath *is an avid reader and writer of poetry who writes during his leisure from being a Warehouse Management System Coordinator in Macon, Georgia. His work has appeared in* The Horror Zine, Sirens Call *e-zine and will be appearing in a forthcoming issue of* Infernal Ink.

**SCROOGE** *by Andrew Muff*

Andrew Muff *is a graduate of Rosalind Franklin University of Medicine and Science and works as a physician assistant in Wichita, KS. He is also a short fiction writer and freelance illustrator. His work has previously been published in* Perihelion Science Fiction, Electric Spec, *and* Sword and Sorcery Magazine, *and will appear in future issues of* The Martian Wave *and* The Nine Tales Series.

# THE VISITOR

## Patricia Duremdes

She would show up in slivers, between images of hospital beds and scents of disinfectants, like a sun peering through a fleeting gap in the clouds. Her eyes would flash, still frozen in fear and later on melt in resignation, meeting his without recognition. The manifestation of her impending death, the chill of that night, would overtake him and, for a moment, his arms would feel the dead weight of her body.

The unsettling episodes, however, gradually became more vivid until he was convinced they were no longer just impalpable daydreams. He was reliving that moment -repeatedly. The way her eyes turned to lead before they closed for the last time, the chill that froze over his skin like rime, the burning sensation of his chest as he stood there, as lifeless as the body before him. Every day he would see her die, and along with the moment came the same feelings of horror and panic. The images would bear into his waking mind, submerging him into the false urgency of saving her.

A voice would sometimes accompany the visions -the same voice he heard that night. She would speak his name and nothing more. At times she would show herself, alive in her most vibrant form, and their conversation would always be the same.

"Miss me?" she would ask.

"Is this real?" he would ask back.

She would smile at him, playfully it seemed, and say, "Anything can be real if you want it to be."

He would sigh and give an exasperated nod as an answer.

"Why don't you join me?" She would walk up to him, slowly and cautiously, and reach for his hand. He would usually just look at her and take in as much of her as he could. Then he would watch her form slowly dissipate into nothingness.

It went that way for months, and he comforted himself with the idea that she might not be dead at all, but rather turned into a floating ethereal figure that drifted in and out of his life. He often wondered why their conversations never changed, but he eventually figured that she might not show up again if he said anything else. So he kept playing along, remaining silent whenever she asked him to join her.

At times he felt that he was probably going insane, as he subjected himself to repeatedly shifting from the hysteria and agony of reliving her death to the elation of seeing her well and alive right in front of him. He soon noticed that it took a toll at him when he found himself staring at the inviting abyss below the balcony of an office complex. He was certain that if he could just muster the courage to jump into that abyss he would meet her again.

"Miss me?" he heard her ask.

He turned to look at her. "Is this real?"

"Anything can be real if you want it to be." She smiled at him.

"Yes," he said, "yes, I miss you."

"Why don't you join me?" She walked to him and reached for his hand.

He felt the urge to stay silent. He wanted the conversation to end the way it had always ended, but for some reason he grew tired of it all. "Do you want me to?"

"Only if you want to," she said. She looked surprised, seemingly caught off-handed.

"Who are you?"

With her hand holding his, she slowly led him towards the railings of the balcony. "I can be anyone you want me to be," she answered.

As he walked with her—each step more certain than the last—he felt an abrupt surge of peach and calmness. The busy streets below the balcony suddenly turned into a black oblivion; the balcony into a concrete cliff. Silence ensued. For a moment the world was the cliff they were standing on and the deep abyss beneath them.

"Come jump with me," she said. Her presence was inviting, her warm touch a far cry from the cold grip he last remembered of her.

He knew he wanted to. He was just a step away from the abyss, but he realized it was futile. He didn't want her to confirm it, but he believed it was about time that he faced the truth. "You're not her."

For a while she just stared at him in shock, and then she smiled at him, her eyes gleaming with tears. "You're right. I'm not," she finally said.

He felt her let go of his hand and watched her as she jumped into the abyss. He heaved a heavy sigh and stood there for a while before he realized that he was once again on the balcony of the office complex, listening to the distant sound of vehicles passing by the streets below him. For a moment he felt nothing. Then a sudden feeling of anguish stabbed through his chest like a knife. He mourned for her one last time, for he knew he would never see her again.

Patricia Duremdes *is an English writing instructor at the University of the Philippines, Los Baños. She is also attending graduate school at the same university. She spends a lot of time musing over life's complexities, and she is very fond of painting its most mundane aspects through colorful words and vivid imagery. Her other interests include fashion and travel. Patricia is currently living in Los Baños, Laguna, Philippines.*

# Witch's Hands

### Lisa Lepovetsky

Blue veins snake under skin
paler than magic in a virgin's heart,
wrap themselves round arthritic digits
knuckles like mandrake knees
rising from cold black water in
a swamp where no one else goes.
No one else dares.

Whorls stained from the fruits
of nightshade and hemlock and
the stinging sap of the mad-apple
curl around fingertips topped
by ragged nails with matter
trapped under the crescents
like black grins.

These ancient hands, these
blood-crusted palms are never still,
always alive with the memories
of wishes and pain whispered in ears
long scarred with the desires of
folks too filled with longing
to know they're already dead.

Lisa Lepovetsky *is widely published in both the horror and mystery genres. She holds an MFA in writing and her latest book of dark poetry is* Voices from Empty Rooms *(Alban Lake). She lives in the mountains of Pennsylvania.*

# Roses and Ivy

## Diane Arrelle

I stood outside the toyshop, rubbing my gloved hands together. It was freezing, but then again, it was Christmas Eve. The last customers left, then I entered. The wizened, old man behind the counter frowned. He glanced at the clock, three minutes to six, then turned back to watch the TV over the locked glass cabinet behind him.

I smiled and said, "I know it's closing time, I'll only be a few minutes."

He grunted, always the personable salesman. I knew the greedy bastard would stay open till New Year's Eve if it meant making a buck. I walked to the back and stared at the dolls behind those glass doors. I knew every one of them, longed to hold them once again, to own what was rightfully mine. Well, I waited five long years to buy them back, and three of them were gone, sold to strangers for exorbitant prices. I hoped their new owners cherished them as much as I had.

The proprietor turned from the TV and divided his time between sizing me up, glancing at the wall clock and studying a hangnail. He absently bit the broken fingernail, spitting it on the floor. "Lovely dolls, aren't they? All collectable, all in perfect condition, all worth a small fortune," he cackled.

I smiled. "Yes they are beautiful, a young girl would just love to own them, but you are not selling them for a small fortune. No, you are looking to make a huge fortune off of them." I bent and reached under a shelf, lifting up the prize of the entire Rose Doll Collection, Rose's little sister, Ivy. With a cloth from a bag in my coat pocket, I lovingly wiped her down until she gleamed.

He watched me, bit another nail and realized what I was holding. He spun and looked at the cabinet display. The Ivy Doll was missing from her stand.

He glared at me, "How'd you get that doll, she's not for sale. She was a limited edition tewnty years ago.  There are only a few Ivys left in existence!"

"I know," I said, walked to the counter and put her down. "I just wanted to see her again, she was always my favorite."

He reached for his glasses with one hand and gnawed at his thumb-nail of the other, then he grabbed the doll and studied my face.  "Ah, I remember you, you're that girlie who tried to have me arrested for stealing your dolls."

"You did."

He laughed, a nasty cackle, and rubbed Ivy across his chin for a moment. "Well, I bought 'em fair from your stepmother, and I think, I'll call the police on you now. You broke into my store to get hold of Ivy. Why'd you hide her back there? Why didn't you just take her?"

I smiled. "Because she belongs with the collection.  Anyway, you can't prove I broke in and nothing's missing."

He gnawed on another chipped nail and stared at me. "Just what is it you want? It's past closing, what kind of mind game you playing here?"

I smiled, "I like that, mind game. Exactly!"  Then I nodded, laid three one hundred dollar bills on the counter and went to the door. "Merry Christmas, You should change these cheap locks." I watched him put Ivy back in the case, then he grabbed the money and shouted, "What's this for?"

I didn't answer, I just clasped my gloved hands together and left thinking, *Yeah... mind games, mind crimes.  A battle of wits he was doomed to lose.*

I walked ten blocks to the hospital, my coat barely keeping me warm, but my accomplishment was like a furnace for my soul.  Once there, I headed to the back, and using my key, unlocked the large toxic waste recepticle and threw in my coat with the baggie in the pocket and my plastic lined gloves. The dumpster was half empty, and by tomorrow night it would be teeming from all the holiday accidents and emergencies, and the day after that, it would be emptied.

Yes, this Christmas was for me and Dad, God rest his soul. Half a decade ago, that vicious witch married him for his money, then dis-covered he was just a poor, sick man with a teen-age daughter. I went off to college and she sold everything we owned, including the house. She even sold my Rose doll collection for three-hundred dollars. Dad used to buy me a doll every Christmas and birthday. I loved them so much, and had planned to give them to my daughters when I had a family.

That bitch ran off and Dad died penniless. I struggled and worked and finally graduated nursing school. She ended up in the ER on my shift last Christmas Eve just like a present. Poor woman died, I mean, who could've known she was allergic to penicillin?

This year, I worked in the infectious disease ward, and decided to give myself another Christmas present. My little Ivy, wiped with the cloth that had been soaked in all sorts of deadly germs and bacteria, had become Poison Ivy for the night. That nail biting creep should be feeling pretty sick about now. By the end of my shift, he'll be dead and no one will even know he was murdered. I smiled at the thought. Wow, another easy death and I'm the only one who will ever know it, just my own little mind crime. I'll pop on over there tomorrow to collect and clean up my purchase. It will be good to have my Roses and Ivy back home for the holidays.

Dina Leacock *writing under the name Diane Arrelle has sold more than two-hundred short stories and two books including* Just A Drop In The Cup, *a collection of short-short stories. She recently retired from being director of a municipal senior citizen center and resides with her husband, her younger son and her cat on the edge of the Pine Barrens (home of the Jersey Devil)*

# I DO

*John Tustin*

She spits out my name like a peppercorn that dared to enter
her mouth because it failed to dissolve in the soup.

I cut myself and she pleads that I not stain
the new carpet.

She tells me she hates me as I put the kids
to bed.

She uses my balls for target practice
and wears my dignity as a choker at family gatherings.

She prays for my death to red-eyed gods with the heads
of hyenas,
offering them strands of my hair wrapped
in a fifty dollar bill.

She dreams of dragging my lifeless body down the
basement steps,
my head clunk clunking on each
scabby wooden plank.

My books molder in the basement.
My poems spy from their hidey-hole in the rafters.
My music whispers from a far off room.
My love lies dormant, waiting for another.

She poisons the minds of my children
as she fouls the air with the inference
of her movements.

I sit like a statue, eyes glazed,
heart scarring over, cut open,
scarring over again and again.

Waiting for what's next.

I write it down and she burns it.

I speak it and she shoves the words back into mouth,
complaining about the stink of my breath
and the yellowness of my teeth
as she shoves.

I wear it and she strips it
from me.

I S.O.S. by blinking my eyes
and she pulls the eyelashes out one by one,
blowing them into the nether,
wishing the evil wishes of greedy czarinas
as the lashes float into the obscurity
of rugs and desks and ignored windowsills and freshly
painted walls.

And I sit like a statue,
staring at my beautiful children,
waiting for what's next.

Ever since I said I Do,
I can't.

John Tustin *is currently exiled in Elba.* fritzware.com/johntustinpoetry
*is a link to his poetry online.*

# TO YOUR BODIES SCATTERED GO

## Manfred Gabriel

The blackout rolled through the city in violent waves. Building by building, street by street, neighborhood by neighborhood. The industrial towers of charred steel, the concrete tenements, the traffic signals at congested intersections. Every street lamp, every storefront, every blinking cell tower. All of it awash in darkness.

For a few moments, the headlamps of cabs and busses, cars and motorbikes, were the only light, buoys adrift on a turbulent sea, their horns the only sound. Then, the wave receded. For a few moments, the lights came back on, reflecting brightly off the ever-present shroud of gray that was the sky. But soon enough, the wave rolled back in, and the city darkened once again.

Val could not see any of this from the overseer's station, but he could tell what was happening by watching the readouts on the monitors, as easy as a blind man reading brail. He contacted the Reclamation Centers in outlying suburbs for more power, but received the usual reply — "We're short, too, Val, awaiting a new load."

Finally, Train 472 rolled into the Reclamation Center, steam pouring from its stacks, pulling behind it a long line of freight cars tarnished with soot. Val could just make out the engineer, his face masked. He waved to Val and went about his work.

The train slowed to a crawl alongside a wide chute. As each car passed, its roof opened, and it dumped its cargo down onto the chute, letting gravity take it down to the furnaces. When the train was empty, it hurried off to pick up a new load.

A flu pandemic raged across the city. The war continued. There was no shortage of fuel, only a shortage of the means to get it where it needed to go.

Val counted the cars as they rolled away. Fifty-two freight cars. Another four hours of energy. He checked the monitors to ensure that the fuel was reaching the furnaces, that the BTU's were rising. He snacked on a fiber bar, bland but a meal was a meal, sipped his coffee – the real stuff. His position had its privileges.

A voice buzzed in Val's ear. Ulah, his chief engineer. "Better get down here," she said.

"You know I can't leave the station," Val replied. Ulah was always bothering him with some make-believe crises or another.

"It's important. You gotta see this."

Val hesitated. Ulah insisted once more. Finally, he acquiesced.

Setting his monitors on automatic to let him know if the furnaces fell below approved norms, he left his station and hurried down the hall, the door sealing behind him with a sharp hiss. The hall gave way to a narrow metal walkway with rusted railings on either side. Below him, the turbines whirred, the sound deafening. Powered by the furnaces, they generated the electricity which kept the city plugging along. He headed down a set of steps to the main floor. He took another corridor past the furnaces. They roared. The heat stifled. Through heavy glass, he saw the fires burning orange and red with a hint of blue. For a moment, he thought he saw a blackened skull amongst the flames. He blinked at it was gone.

Ulah stood next to the conveyor belt that led from the chutes to the furnaces. On the belt were thousands of bodies. Infants and children, adults in what should have been the prime of their lives, but mostly the aged, withered and frail, stripped naked, some stiff with rigor mortis. Every one of them were fuel for the fires.

The belt should have been moving, but it wasn't.

"I shut her down," Ulah said, shouting above the roar of the furnaces. She was a sturdy woman, short, with broad shoulders, her long hair kept beneath a cap.

"Without my say so?" Val said. She often made decisions without his approval. Would have gotten her fired long ago if she wasn't usually right.

"Look." She pointed to a spot towards the center of the belt. At first, Val saw nothing, then Ulah shined her light at a hand sticking straight up in the air. Nothing unusual. Bodies landed every which way, landed it a chaotic tangle. It didn't matter. They burned all the same.

The hand moved.

"A death spasm," Val said.

Ulah shook her head. "Been doing that since before I called you."

Val lept up onto the belt, tried but failed to step between the bodies. He stumbled along the legs and arms and torsos, like they were rocks along the shore. He heard a bone crack beneath his heavy boot. His ankle got caught in the armpit of another body, his leg twisted and he fell. He found himself face-to-face with an old woman, shriveled, wide-eyed. Picking himself up, he finally reached the hand. A man's hand, the arm thick and muscled with an eagle tattoo dark black against pale skin. The palm was calloused, dirt beneath cracked fingernails. Val rolled a couple of other bodies out of the way so that he could get a good look at the res of him. He was not large, but he was young and trim. His blonde hair was cut short, his eyes closed. His lips retained the slightest bit of color. Val squatted, felt for a pulse, listened to his chest, put his hand in front of the nose and mouth. The pulse was there, but faint.

Val hoisted the body up on his shoulders, lugged it off the belt. He laid the man flat, checked for his pulse again, but didn't find it.

Ulah turned away. "Holy shit," she said. "Holy shit." Val hauled the body back onto the belt, ordered it turned back on. The furnaces had to be fed.

The mover slid along its steel track, beyond sprawling, half-abandoned suburbs and out across the sands. A hard wind blew, whipping up dervishes that spun high into the shrouded sky.

The Dome gleamed in the distance, growing ever-larger as the mover approached. Val had a pretty good idea why the Director had summoned him. His handheld beeped. Ulah letting him know a new trainload had arrived. None living, though, not that she could see. None since that one, almost a week ago.

The mover slipped beneath an archway crisscrossed with laser lights, entering the Dome.

Flat roofed buildings built into low green hills. Lilacs bloomed. Groves of birch and oak and pine towered overhead. Sunlight filtered through the dome, free of gray, revealing its true warmth, its true light.

The mover halted in front of a building that seemed to be all windows, curved to form a courtyard where corporates sat drinking their morning coffee and tapping away on handhelds. The double doors slid open as Val approached. A receptionist standing in the lobby greeted him with a friendly smile, asked him to wait. He couldn't help noticing the long slit that ran up the length of her skirt.

Val sank into an oversized chair. A screen wall opposite him displayed images of the Dome with a caption that read – Tomorrow's Eden: Without the Forbidden Fruit. After a few minutes, a man greeted him. Not the Director, but his Assistant, Ferrol. He had dark skin and spoke with a slight accent Val could not place. His suit was neatly pressed, his teeth gleamed white. His eyes were the deepest shade of blue, his fingernails manicured. As Val rose to shake hands with him, he noted how short the Assistant Director was.

Ferrol led Val down a wide corridor, greeting other workers as they passed, with a wide smile and hearty hellos. He knew each one by name.

The corridor ended in a conference room much too large for a two person meeting. Two of the walls were lined floor to ceiling with windows. "We paid enough for the sunlight," Ferrol explained. "We may as well take advantage of it."

They sat across from each other at one end of a long conference table. A boy brought them water, clean and filtered. "The Director is sorry he could not be here himself."

"That's okay," Val said. He was glad the Director was not there. It meant the situation may not be as serious as he originally thought.

Ferrol pulled his handheld from his inside jacket pocket, studied it a moment. Val could not see the screen, but had a feeling it was his work file. "You've done a fine job for us, a fine job. So tell me, why would you want to ruin it?"

"I was only trying to make you aware of the situation. We never had a live body come through before."

"That you know of."

"That I know of, yes."

Ferrol slipped the handheld back into his pocket, rose, walked over to the windows. He stared out at the lush lawn that sloped to a grove of trees where a narrow creek ran. "We have precautions in place," he said. "Still, it happens."

Val tried not to look surprised. "But the dead, they come from morgues. Some have been autopsied, all are required to have death certificates."

Ferrol turned, smiled, all teeth. "Have you ever visited a shrine?"

Val's parents had died long before the reclamation centers began to be used to fuel the city. They lay in a grave in a cemetery in the small town in which they grew up, on land that had no value for anything else. He had no other close family, none who had died, anyway. So he had never had a reason to visit a shrine.

They took Ferrol's private car out of the dome, humming down a road that ran alongside the mover's rails. The city rose up in the distance ahead of them, towers jutting into the sky like stalagmites in a dark cave.

They turned off the road and parked on a dusty field next to a cluster of other private cars. There was a mover station, a few people waited on the platform for the next ride.

The two men walked down a set of spiral steps. They passed through a gate that scanned them as they entered. There were no guards to be seen.

The cavern walls and ceiling were programmed to depict an early morning sky. Not the soot filled one of reality, or the filtered one of the dome. This was an idealized sky, like one might imagine on a cool fall morning, foggy with a hazy sun overhead. People stood at stations made to look like items found in nature – a tree, a rock, even a bubbling stream. They placed their palms on these stations, and before them would stand the perfect, holographic figure of an old man, a young woman, a small child. Someone they had loved and lost, without the imperfections, the illnesses, the scars the wounds. Perfect.

The holographs could not speak. They did not move. They could not be touched. Still, people would talk to them, try to hug them. Some cried. Some stood silent. After a few minutes, the holograph would disappear and they would leave. Whether they felt better or worse, Val could not say.

Val and Ferrol strolled along a path that wove between the stations. Ferrol stopped at a bench, but did not sit down. Neither did Val.

"The corporation built this place, when the first reclamation center opened." Ferrol did not lower his voice when he said this. "As a way to make up for the cemeteries, the mausoleums that had been lost."

Val did not say anything. It wasn't anything he didn't already know.

"It is in fact better. No tombstones or plaques as the only thing to remember the dearly departed by. No, you can actually see them, not as they were, but as they should have been."

They walked a little further. Ferrol kept his hands behind his back. "Do you notice something? Look at how few people are here."

"Perhaps they don't think this is a good substitute."

Val frowned, shook his head. "We've done surveys, studies. People just don't care. Oh, they say it matters. There is something about "disgracing" the dead that bothers them. But it's only the idea of it, not the reality. Especially if it means keeping the lights on, ensuring they are cool on a hot summer's day.

"Still, we are in a precarious situation. We can't underestimate our position. If what you found got out, the narrowsphere would have a field day, even if we could control the mass media. There would be protests, new regulations, maybe even pressure to shut down. We couldn't have that. The world could not have that."

They were heading back up the stairs. Ferrol put a hand on Val's shoulders. "Sometimes, errors happen."

"It's a big error."

"We have been keeping an eye on you," Ferrol said. "You have potential. A promotion maybe. But we need people who are loyal. Who play by the rules. Do you understand?"

They were above ground again. A mover had pulled up. A few people got off and on. "You can take the mover back to the city, back to your job. Or you could come with me, back to the Dome. Sunshine. Clean air. Which will it be?"

Something was wrong with the data.

Val sat in his cushioned office, sunlight streaming. A screen rose from the center of the room, displaying real-time data for the six reclamation centers under his supervision. He had been Supervising Director for a little over three months, given a tidy bungalow on the edge of the dome. Long walks on wooded paths after leisurely suppers in the commissary. No more furnaces, no more heat, no more bodies – just numbers on the screen. Numbers which didn't add up.

It would have been imperceptible to most of his peers. Kids just out of grad school with a knack for number crunching and practical physics, but no real world experience. They had never witnessed the dead rolling by on conveyor belts, except perhaps on their orientation tour. He checked and rechecked his figures. Fewer and fewer bodies were going in, but more and more electricity was going out.

"I've been reading your logs," Ferrol said. They were sitting at one of the café tables outside the office building, a demitasse of espresso in front of him. Val drank coffee. A bot rolling by every few moments to refill their cups. "Very thorough. You definitely know your business."

"Thank you," Val managed to say.

"But about these numbers in your last log, you are sure they are correct?"

"I verified them with each overseer."

"Did they say anymore?"

"They gave me only the information I asked for."

"And you didn't find that odd?"

"I was one of them, but I'm new. They don't know my motives."

"And what are your motives?"

"I'm just verifying and reporting the data, sir," Val said.

Ferrol ran a hand through his hair. "Our integrity is everything. If people suspect …"

"This is internal information only."

Ferrol patted Val on the shoulder. "Good, then I'll look into it."

Val sat on the small patio outside his bungalow, enjoying the sound of crickets chirping, the blinking of fireflies flitting through the air, the smell of freshly mown grass. Little things he hadn't experienced since he was a boy. Little things he never thought he'd experience again.

A message came over his handheld. It was Ulah. "We have to meet."

Before his promotion, Val lived on the seventh floor of tenement 132. A u-shaped building made of concrete blocks and a dirt courtyard where the children played soccer with a weathered ball.

It was here Ulah told him to come. She knew he had lived here, knew no one would take much notice of him. But she was late. Val stood uncomfortably at one corner, near a first floor window, curtained and barred. He could hear a purifier humming inside.

"At least you could've dressed down a little," Ulah said. She was still in her work overalls, even though her shift had long ended.

"It's all I have anymore," Val replied. He had remained in contact with Ulah since he left, sending her packages with perks from the dome – orange juice, chocolate, basil and asparagus. It was only after he left that he found, despite their differences at work, they were both dedicated, that she had been his only friend. He had her promoted to replace him as overseer when he left.

Ulah looked him up and down, "Can I still trust you?"

"I haven't changed that much."

Ulah took him by the hand, which surprised him. They had never more than shaken hands. As they walked down the street, he realized that it was so no one would look at them twice. A couple in love, not a worker off to show her superior something she would not speak of over the handhelds, or even in public. "You have to see," she said.

The plant was not far. One of the few things Val had liked about his tenement was that it was within walking distance to work. They entered through the employee entrance. "I jammed the eyes and the infrareds, but we don't have much time before someone notices."

Ulah released his hand, led him down the narrow corridor, the caged lights above them flickering.

They reached a gangway that spanned the conveyor belt. Val stopped.

The belt was full, but not with bodies. They were people, upright and apparently still alive.

"They started showing up a few days ago." Ulah sat with Val in her studio apartment, a small window overlooked the city's gray skyline. A light that might have been mistaken for a sunset, peaked over the buildings, but it was only the light of the distant dome. "I think they drug them before they show up, otherwise, there'd be panic."

The people stood in disorderly rows, blank stares on their faces. They walked along the conveyer belt slow, zombie like. They were all still clothed. Some wore hospital gowns. Still more were clad in the lime green pajamas worn by inmates at the urban holding facility, the monolithic building which held the thousands awaiting trial in a backlogged system. They stepped willingly into the great furnace, not even bothering to whimper, let alone scream, as the flames engulfed them.

"What should we do?" Ulah asked. They were in the observation room. She had made some of the tea Val had sent her a few days before. Val wasn't drinking. He stared into it, as if though he might find answers there.

"I'll go to Ferrol," Val said finally. "You lay low. No sense in two of us putting our necks out."

"You have more to lose."

"Which is why I should be the one. Besides. I have access."

"He could be in on it. Maybe we should hit the narrowsphere. We can take vid. Post."

"No," Val replied. "No one would believe it. We have to fix this from the inside." Val said. He pulled out his handheld, began typing a meeting request.

Ferrol's automated aid, a tube of glimmering haze, told Val its boss was out, that it didn't know when he would be back. Val ignored it, walked into the office, the double doors making way as he entered. The AD had not replied to his meeting request.

The office was three times the size of Val's. A seating area included psueather chairs and a long sofa. Ferrol sat down in one of the chairs. Every now and then, the aid would roll in, ask if he needed anything. When Val asked when Ferrol would be back, the aid had no answer.

"I'm afraid Mr. Smythe is no longer with us."

Val turned to see a tall older man with a silver mane came down over his suit collar. Val recognized him as the Director himself. Broad shouldered with close cropped hair and narrow eyes. He sat in one of the chairs across from Val. The director held up a handheld.

"Ferrol got your message. We did, too."

"Where is he?"

"Transferred."

"Just like that?" Val was surprisingly calm face to face with a man who could shut off the lights with a snap of his fingers. On his way here, he thought about what the company had done, decided he just didn't care about anything else anymore.

"Just like that."

"He tried to do something about it then."

"That's important to you?"

"I like to know if my instincts were correct, if I was right to trust him."

"You can trust all of us," The Director said. "You have been with us, what, twenty some years? You should know by now. We aren't some stereo typical evil corporation from a twentieth century thriller. We aren't the bad guys."

"You burn them alive."

The Director walked around the desk, leaned on it as he spoke. "The War is winding down. Fewer troops are dying on the battlefields. Fewer POWs are dying in makeshift camps. The pandemic has run its course. We are running short of supply. These bodies, they aren't alive, not really. Prisoners, indigents, incurable drug addicts. Plagues on society. Of no value to society. Soon to die in some prison cell or on the executioner's table or in some alleyway anyway. We are only accelerating the process."

Val thought about this. "But alive?"

"Easier to transport. They can walk on their own two feet. Don't worry. They feel nothing, the gas pumped into the freight cars makes sure of that."

"Murder," Val said under his breath.

"Efficiency," The Director replied. "I know how you feel. It took me some time to come to this conclusion. All human life has equal value. That was what they taught us at home, at church, in school. But that was before, when we had the luxury to be compassionate. It's different now. To be human is not enough. You must have purpose."

Val did not say anything to that. He watched a bird perch on a tree outside. He thought it had the dull coloring of a female cardinal, but he could not be sure. It had been a long time since he had seen one. The Director seemed to notice it to, he turned, went to the windows, stood looking out with his hands behind his back.

"This dome is a model," he said. "Our technology has almost destroyed this world. Our technology will bring it back. Someday, we will be able to abandon the cities, let the earth retake them, while we enjoy lives in Edens such as this. But not everyone. No, there is not room for everyone."

"Where does that leave me?"

"You, you have value. You are smart, capable. It would be a shame to use you to fuel our new world. We do not want to. As I said, we are not monsters. But those who remain, they must not only be strong of mind and body, they must be strong in spirit as well. They must want to belong."

"And Ulah?"

"She has her value as well, but she does not have spirit." The Director looked around the room. "This is a nice office. And we need a new Assistant Director. This time, we will not make the mistake of keeping the dream from him, however. He will know all there is to know. He already does." The Director met Val's gaze. He had eyes of icy blue. "Think about it."

The sun was just beginning to go down. It shined through the dome, through the office windows. How he had missed the sun. His decision was made.

Val shuffled with the crowd towards the fire, so hot against his face. He tried to will himself to stop walking, stop moving, but his feet would not slow down.

His new office was so comfortable, and the sun so very bright.

Manfred Gabriel's *short fiction has appeared in numerous publications, most recently* Bastion SF, Under a Dark Sign *and* Triptych Tales. *He has written essays for* History is Now Magazine *and his musings on the modern workplace can be found at www.highschoolwithmoney.com. He lives and writes in western Wisconsin with his wife, three daughters, and a menagerie of animals, including a chinchilla, two dogs who act more like cats and two cats who act more like dogs.*

# ORGAN VENTURES

## WC Roberts

pay the cash and wait for the knife
market off the spare parts
up for sale—a kidney please?
—it's an universal match

a retina, maybe the whole eye
don't use it to unlock any doors
a finger?  I had ten…
that print was mine—a  at one time

the offer is limited
so come shop while the goods are in
need a liver? the price is for half
a—it'll grow back

come in for a visit
one lump or two
it's a steal, I say,
whispering over cups of tea

come with the cash, I'm not picky
euros, pounds, dollars
what difference does it make
just make it cash
they'd only trip us up.
let's dance

WC Roberts *lives in a mobile home up on Bixby Hill, on land that was once the county dump. The only window looks out on a ragged scarecrow standing in a field of straw and dressed in WC's own discarded clothes. WC dreams of the desert, of finally getting his first television set, and of ravens. Above all, he writes, and has had poems published in* Bete Noire, Strange Horizons, Apex, Space & Time Magazine, Mindflights, Aoife's Kiss, Big Pulp, Star\*Line, *and others.*

**BLINK AWAKE** *by Eleanor Leonne Bennett*

Eleanor Leonne Bennett is an internationally award winning artist of almost fifty awards. She was the CIWEM Young Environmental Photographer of the Year in 2013. Eleanor's photography has been published in British Vogue and Harper's Bazaar. Her work has been displayed around the world consistently for six years since the age of thirteen. This year (2015) she has done the anthology cover for the incredibly popular Austin International Poetry Festival. She is also featured in Schiffer's "Contemporary Wildlife Art" published this Spring. She is also a senior art editor.

# EVEN IMAGINARY FRIENDS NEED SOMEONE TO PLAY WITH

## Robin White

The hangover which woke Hajime was the worst of his life. Overnight, his brain had turned to sludge, oozing out of his nose and leaking from his ears. His head stuck to the pillow, his eyelids fused shut and his belly was a poisonous reservoir of recrimination.

He flung out an arm to find the clock, opening his eyes wide enough to make out the digital red numbers, blinking at him accusingly. It was after 11 in the morning.

"Shit," he said.

Rolling, rather than standing off the bed, Hajime crawled into the bathroom and leant over the toilet, hacking and coughing and willing himself to puke, with zero end-result. He turned round, sat down and tried to remove the poison another way. No luck. He ran the cold tap and leant to the side, letting as much of it fall into his open mouth as possible.

The shower, once he'd made his way into it, was impossibly hot. Somebody, potentially him, must have messed with the faucet. Turning it too far the other way, a blast of frigid water him in the face, bending him over out of its grasp. The exertion made him vomit.

"Oh shit," he said.

"Hajime San," said Mr. Hideo. "Thank you so much for joining us."

Hajime bowed low. "I am sorry, Mr. Hideo. I had problems at home and-"

"I'm sure they were very important. But if you could, I'd like you to sit down now, and join us."

Rushing to a seat, Hajime looked around the table. There was no-body else at its mahogany top but himself and Mr. Hideo. He shook his head and blinked away several layers of blurry confusion.

"Us, Mr. Hideo?"

"That's right. You see only me, for the moment, am I right?"

Hajime nodded. "Yes, sir. Is there somebody else?"

"Seated to my right," gestured Mr. Hideo, "is Fumiko. I am in love with her."

"Fumiko, sir?"

"That's what I said."

Hajime blinked. "But there's nobody there."

"Well," said Mr. Hideo, "Fumiko is imaginary, Hajime San."

"Imaginary?"

"Quite. She lives in my brain. She's my imaginary friend."

Hajime wrinkled his forehead and scratched his chin. If Mr. Hideo went insane, he wondered, would he get control of the department?

"You're joking with me."

"Not at all. I am telling you that my imaginary friend, a beautiful woman with light brown eyes and curly hair, is sat to my right at this very moment. I am telling you that her name is Fumiko and I am tell-ing you that she is imaginary. This is not a joke, and if you persist in assuming that it is, I will have you fired."

Hajime gaped.

"I suppose you're wondering why I'm telling you this?" asked Mr. Hideo.

"Yes, a little bit."

"Because you are to take a business trip to Tokyo this afternoon, and Fumiko will go with you."

"Mr. Hideo?"

"You will be meeting with Ryuusei Takagawa, a property develop-er, who wishes to build on spare land we own just outside of Kobe. This is no small deal, Hajime and if you succeed in bartering it, you will have won my trust, and I will make you next-in-line to head the division."

Hajime thought about it. "I need to bring Fumiko with me?"

"Yes."

"I need to bring your imaginary friend, Fumiko, with me?"

"Yes."

"How?"

"You'll be flying. Your flight leaves at 3 o'clock, so you'd better go home and get your things."

"And Fumiko?"

"Fumiko doesn't have any things," said Mr. Hideo. "She's imaginary."

Hajime disliked flying, and was pleased to occupy himself during take-off with Mr. Hideo's list of instructions. They were brief.

- You are to meet with Ryuusei Takagawa and finalise negotiations for the proposed build on our Kobe land.
- You are to treat Fumiko with the utmost respect at all times.
- You are not to touch Fumiko, nor let her touch you.
- You will enquire as to Fumiko's health every hour, on the hour.
- Her happiness is of paramount importance. She wishes to see Tokyo, and you will take her wherever she wants to go.

Hajime checked his watch, and waited until it struck the hour. He had seven minutes to spare, and he used them to order a vodka & orange juice. It was delicious, but not strong enough. He ordered another.

At 4PM, Hajime turned to the empty seat beside him and asked if it was okay. The seat, filled by an imaginary person, said nothing.

"Is there anywhere," Hajime asked the empty seat, "you'd like to see in particular once we reach Tokyo?"

He ordered another vodka & orange juice, drank it quickly, loosened his tie and occupied himself with the in-flight magazine until landing.

Hajime's cell phone buzzed inside his jacket pocket whilst waiting for a taxi at Haneda airport. Turning to his left, he asked Fumiko if she'd answer it for him. Receiving no reply, he answered it himself.

"Hajime Wakahisa. How can I help?

It was a woman's voice on the other end of the line. From the sound of it, breathy, and high-pitched, she was young. Barely out of college.

"I'm calling on behalf of Mr. Takagawa's office in Tokyo," she said. "You are no longer required to meet with Mr. Takagawa. The negotiations have been concluded. Thank you for your trip."

"What? But I-"

"Mr. Hideo has requested that you stay in Tokyo for the evening, and show your guest the sights."

"My guest?"

"Yes. Miss. Fumiko."

"All right. To whom am I speaking?"

The line went dead, or the woman hung up. Hajime sighed.

His taxi driver was a genial fellow, a little overweight and with big, thick moustache. He had a little American flag in the backseat, hanging from a coat hook. Hajime had long wanted to travel to the United States, and asked the taxi driver if he'd been.

"No. But I'd like to. I'm into American music."

"Really? What kind?"

"Film scores, mostly."

"Oh? What films?"

"I love the music to Star Wars. And Indiana Jones. E.T. You know, the classics."

Hajime nodded. "I love those movies."

"Oh, I've never seen the movies," said the taxi driver. "I just love the scores."

"Why's that?"

The driver shrugged. "They feel more real to me than the pictures."

"I've never paid them that much attention."

"You should, if you ever get the chance. Hey, we'll be at your hotel soon."

"Thanks."

The streets of Tokyo were brighter than Kobe, a sea of flashing neon, corporate logos and illicit delights. Hajime hoped he'd get a chance to sample the nightlife. Bar Eleven, in the *Roppongi* district, was famous for its attractive clientele. He might meet a girl.

"You here alone?"

Hajime laughed.

"What? Why are you laughing?"

"Because I'm here with an imaginary friend," he said.

The driver stared at him in the rear-view mirror. "Your imaginary friend?"

"Not mine. My boss's imaginary friend."

"Ah. Well that's different."

"How is that different?"

"It just is. I thought you were here with your own imaginary friend, like you were some kind of weirdo. But you're doing a favour for your boss. That makes sense."

"But she's still imaginary."

The driver thought about it. "But she's not in your imagination, is she?"

"I suppose not."

"So you don't know what she looks like?" asked the taxi driver.

"Nope," said Hajime. "I guess I don't."

"Well," said the taxi driver, pulling over at the hotel, "I can tell you what she looks like."

"You can? How?"

"I can see her. She's imaginary, is all."

"Right."

"So I can see her."

"Of course. So what does she look like?"

"At the moment, she looks a little pissed off. Have you asked her how she is?"

"I haven't. I was supposed to at 5PM. Guess I messed up."

"Well ask her soon. And hey, buddy."

"Yes?"

The driver lowered his voice. "She's got great cans."

⋘✠⋙

At 6PM, Hajime flicked off the TV in his hotel room and thought about dinner. Looking at the empty pillow next to him, he asked it how it was doing. The pillow, being used by an imaginary person, said nothing.

"Good talk," he said. "Is there anything in Tokyo you'd like to see? We could. Oh. Hang on."

The phone on his bedside table was ringing. Expecting Mr. Hideo, Hajime answered with a respectful note in his voice.

"Is that Hajime?"

It was was the same woman again.

"Yes. This is Hajime. Is the meeting back on?"

"No."

"Oh."

There was silence, except for her breathing on the other end of the line.

"Hello?"

"Yes?"

"Who am I talking to, please?" asked Hajime.

"Who would you like to be talking to?"

"Excuse me?"

"It's me," said the voice.

"Who?"

"I've been with you all afternoon."

"...Fumiko?"

"Yes."

"Is this a joke?"

"No."

"But you're imaginary."

"So?" she said. "Imagine me."

Hajime shook his head. "This doesn't make any sense. This has to be a joke."

"The phone you're holding is grey."

"What?"

"I can see that the phone you're holding is grey."

He looked at it. "A lot of phones are grey," he said. "That doesn't prove anything."

"The wallpaper in your room is beige. The carpet is light green, and has a swirly pattern. You're wearing a navy-blue suit, and red socks. On the bedside table is your copy of the in-flight magazine, which you took so that you could finish the crossword. You're turned on by my voice, and have an erection."

Hajime looked down. It wasn't quite an erection, but it was mostly there.

"Don't say anything. Just lie still."

"What's going on?"

"Just lie there and listen to my voice."

"What are you going to do?"

"We're going to have sex."

"But you're imaginary!"

"So," said Fumiko. "Imagine me."

After they had finished, Hajime, set down the phone, pulled up his pants and fastened his belt. One of his socks had come off, and he retrieved it from under the bed. The phone rang again as he was putting it on.

"Fumiko?"

"Yes."

"That was the best sex I've ever had."

"It always is, with me. It's one of the perks of being imaginary."

She sounded sad. Hajime wasn't sure what to do.

"Are you okay?"

"I just. Ugh."

"What?"

"I wish I wasn't alone," she said. "Being imaginary is so lonely."

"But so many people can imagine you."

"Yes. But none of them really see me."

"Mr. Hideo does."

She snapped. "Don't talk about Mr. Hideo to me."

"He cares about you."

"No," said Fumiko. "He doesn't care about me at all. He imagined me in the first place. Did you know that? I'm his imaginary friend. But he won't imagine any more friends for me. He just imagines me when he needs me and lets me float away into nothingness otherwise."

"Would you like me to talk to him for you?"

"No! You musn't. He's dangerous, Hajime."

"Mr. Hideo?" Hajime laughed. "He's not dangerous, he's an old man. He's going to give me his department."

There was a pause. "Is he?" asked Fumiko.

"Yes."

"Why would he do that?"

"I'm a good worker."

"Are you?"

"I'm better than most," Hajime said.

"Sometimes, yes. But you drink too much. And you're late, a lot. And he doesn't like the way you dress. Too non-traditional."

Hajime bridled. "Now listen," he said. "I like a drink, and I'm late every so often, and I suppose I dress a little eccentrically, but I'm going to be his replacement. I'll be head of the department."

"Don't get upset."

"I'm not upset."

"You're shouting at an imaginary person."

"I'm not shouting."

"Just be careful with Mr. Hideo. He's not all he seems."

"Fumiko..."

"Promise me you'll be careful."

"All right." Hajime nodded. "I'll be careful."

"Good," said Fumiku. "That's good. I wouldn't want anything to happen to you."

Hajime, still with one sock off, had a thought. "Could we have sex again?"

"All right," said Fumiku. "But this time, imagine we're using protection."

❧✠☙

"Hajime-San" said Mr. Hideo. "How was your trip?"

Hajime smiled, bowed and waved away the offered cup of green tea.

"Fine, thank you, Mr. Hideo. A little pointless, though."

"How so?"

"The meeting with Mr. Takagawa was called off."

"Yes, the negotiations were concluded early. But the trip wasn't a waste of time, I hope. How was Fumiko? Did you get along?"

Hajime nodded. "Yes, sir."

"Ever though she's imaginary?"

"Yes, sir."

"And did you follow my rules?"

Hajime's gut shifted. He smiled through the discomfort. "Yes, sir."

"Did you show her any of the sights?"

"She didn't ask to see any."

"That's unlike her," said Mr. Hideo. "Do you take whiskey?"

"Whiskey, sir?"

"I can smell alcohol on your breath, Hajime, and I'm wondering if you're a whiskey man."

Hajime took a step backwards. "I'm so sorry, Mr. Hideo. I had a drink with lunch, is all."

Mr. Hideo grinned. "Don't apologise. I'm not angry, just curious. What do you drink?"

"Well, I suppose, if you're asking, I mostly drink vodka."

"With tonic?"

"I prefer orange juice."

"I only have tonic. Will that do?"

"Now, sir?"

Mr. Hideo nodded, held up a little bottle of tonic and tipped it all into a crystal tumbler, which was already half-filled with a clear spirit. He offered it to Hajime. "Here," he said.

"Thank you, sir."

"Drink up."

"Are you having one?"

"Of course," said Mr. Hideo. He poured himself a large whiskey, the cheapest *Nikka* brand, and sank it one gulp.

Hajime almost laughed, thinking about Fumiko's warning. He wasn't the only drinker, it would seem. "Cheers," he said, and sank his own cocktail. It tasted a little odd, but tonic always had to him. He preferred the sweetness of juice.

"So, Hajime. You might want to sit down."

"Sir?"

"I've news for you."

"Am I to take your place?"

"Please, Hajime. Sit."

Hajime took a seat on a broad leather sofa which ran along one side of the office. Unable to contain his excitement, he leaned forward in his chair.

"You are a lot like me, Hajime. And not just in personality, but looks, too. The same hairline, same nose, same jaw. We even wear a similar goatee."

"We do, sir."

"There is a difference, however."

"Sir?"

Mr. Hideo sat himself down behind his desk. "I, Hajime, know when to follow rules."

Hajime leant back, furrowing his brow.

"Rules?"

"You broke my rules, Hajime-San."

"Mr. Hideo, I didn't break your rules." He paused to rub a hand against his temple. It had begun to ache, a dull thing behind his eyes.

"You assaulted Fumiko."

"Mr. Hideo! I did not."

"You sexually assaulted my imaginary friend, Hajime."

"This is ridiculous!" Hajime tried to stand, but found his field of vision blurry. Two pairs of hands took him by either elbow. Rolling his head to either side, he saw that they wore police uniforms.

"You can't have me arrested for assaulting your imaginary friend! Besides," he said, through sloppy lips, "she started it!"

Mr. Hideo held a hand in the air, stopping the policemen from taking Hajime away. "Why would she do that?" he asked.

"Because she wanted another friend. She was lonely!"

"Oh. Well."

"Please, call off the police," said Hajime.

"They're already gone."

Hajime realised the pressure on his elbows had subsided. His head sank back on his shoulders. His eyelids had never felt so heavy.

"The police are imaginary," said Mr. Hideo. "But that's okay. Because so are you."

And Hajime popped out of existence.

Robin White *lives in New York City with his wife, Wesley. His work has appeared in the likes of the* Saturday Evening Post, Strangelet, *and* Dogzplot, *among others. He is twenty-seven.*

# In The Aftermath Of Detroit's Apocalypse

## Florence Grey

All that remain are the tattered remnants of my city.
Her soul, her spirit, is lost—
Lost to the politics of time,
to the ravages of ignorance,
and mischance.
Only her ghost still lingers here.
Still haunting the familiar places I once found her.
Frayed relics of The Corridor,
The lingering shadows echo along Cass,
their voices of the
artists, musicians, and beat writers, now silent—
burned out and beaten down like the rest of city.
The once great Siren, you can still hear her injured calls inside
The halls of the Masonic Temple,
The boarded ruins of Creem Magazine that
Pioneered the bohemian city with its bluesy urban rock,
All bare witness to her pitiful demise.
Her streets are littered with the corpses of fallen, burned out icons.
Michigan Central Station, Madison Theater,
The Metropolitan Building,
Will soon be just a memory.
A constant reminder of Detroit's aging beauty, and where it will
Never be again.
Corktown,

Michigan and Trumble,
Vacant—
A concrete wasteland of abandoned cars, homes, and businesses
Of a lost era, the era of hope.
McNichols, Mack, and Outer Drive,
They too are pox marked with
Crack houses,
Burned out houses
abandoned houses,
That were once immigrant houses
At the turn of the last century.
My forbearers,
Immigrants themselves,
Lived on Asbury Park in a place
That, like Detroit, is now in ruins.

Florence Grey *has been writing poetry for nearly twenty years. She loves the swing and big band era and prefers writing her poetry with pen and paper to that of a computer.*

# Pick Me!

## Morgan Shaver

Endless days float past, each one blurring into the other. I cannot remember the day when I was displayed on the high shelf above the produce. Nor can I say with any certainty how long I've been up here. Flanking me are similar creatures, though none of them look much like me. One of them resembles a giant psychopathic sea sponge.

When he was plucked off the shelf his smiling face seemed to regard me with a sick sort of satisfaction. I wasn't fond of him, I wasn't sad to see him go. I was a bit disappointed to see the one who resembled a human girl with short brown hair go. She struck me as friendly, even if we never held a real conversation. I constantly racked my brain for something to say to her, anything at all really.

"Hey, did you see how long the old lady spent picking out three apples?"

Something like that perhaps, but I was never given the chance. As quickly as she had been displayed beside me she was gone. Day after day I waited with anticipation for my turn to be taken home. I'm one of the last, it has to be soon, I can feel it. Unbeknownst to me, I had an uncanny intuition. The following day I notice a flustered-looking gentleman in his mid-twenties walking briskly past the aisles of produce. His hand firmly latched onto a small girl bearing a striking resemblance to the brown-haired creature chosen before me. She holds a bright pink balloon with words written upon it that I cannot read and bounces up and down merrily.

I watch as the gentleman seeks out one of the Workers. The Worker approaches the man and they partake in a deep conversation, frequently pointing in my direction. Excitement flutters within me like papier-mâché in the wind.

"My daughter wants the one that looks like a donkey," the man explains.

"Are you sure? That one is pretty plain. We just got in a lovely light blue one with the characters of Frozen on it. I'm sure she'd like that one better," the Worker responds, preparing to head off to fetch it for the man.

I feel my insides coil. No, I cry to myself, no you must pick me!

"Look, I don't mean to be a pain, but she's got her heart set on that one," the man repeats, pointing once more in my direction.

Yes!

If I could smile I would be beaming as the Worker fetches a ladder and lifts me up off the dusty shelf. My feet leaving four circular imprints behind.

I glance over at the others. A spherical object, another animal shape, I bid them both goodbye. Before I can appreciate my good fortune I find myself in a bag made of paper being transported to the man's home. For several hours I perch on the kitchen counter watching as the family participates in some weird party ritual for the girl. Then, much to my discomfort, I feel the man prying my back open and stuffing it full of what I presume are pieces of candy.

"Daddy, can I hit the piñata first since it's my birthday?" The girl asks tugging the bottom of the man's shirt.

Are they speaking about me? Am I a piñata? If I am, why does she want to hit me? "Sure sweetheart, but don't hit it too hard or it will break and your friends won't get a turn."

The mother of the girl comes in and takes her into the backyard where a dozen additional children have gathered. Their eyes glimmer as they dance over me. The man secures a string tightly around my body and carries me towards a tall tree. Panic courses through me. I try to scream but no sound comes out. I do not want to hang from the tree, I do not want to be hit!

I cannot move, I cannot voice my protests. This is all wrong, it wasn't supposed to end up this way, they were supposed to love and cherish me. I dangle from the tree helpless and full of fear as the man places a white cloth over the girl's eyes. I feel a fleeting glimpse of hope. Her vision is obscured which means she won't be able to find me. I'm safe... right?

But I'm wrong. I am so very wrong.

A glancing blow bounces off my flank before I am forcibly yanked upward out of reach. A sigh of relief escapes me before I am lowered once more. The stick whaps me between the eyes. I feel the pain that only an object approaching its imminent demise can feel. Everything pauses.

There is a pregnant stillness in the air while the man covers another child's face with the cloth. The male child seems more aggressive, his knuckles white as they squeeze the stick. The little girl huddles behind the man with a look of dread. The male child steps forward and WHAM! My belly splits open, candy pouring from the garish wound onto the grass below. Children stream forward screaming triumphantly as they fight and claw and grapple with each other for the candy. The girl wails. Is she crying for me? I wonder.

"Daddy, daddy! It's MY birthday! I was s'posed to break the piñata, it's not fair!" She sobs into the man's shirt as he desperately tries to console her.

A single tear falls from my own face but the man does not comfort me. Instead I am snatched from the tree and cast aside into the garbage.

Morgan Shaver *is a writer, musician, and photographer. She works as a graphic designer and submission strategist for a local small business. Her writing goal is to inspire readers to delve deeper into simple subjects. In her free time she enjoys attending metal concerts, and traveling across the East Coast with her fiancé David. She currently resides in North Arlington, New Jersey.*